ELLA

Diaries

TOP SECRET!

Sara Crawford

With thanks to the Gold Street Primary School
Reading Club — Miette. Aristea. Esther. Alicia. Kitty.
Zac. Robert. Eugenie. Lara. Chloe. Lucy. Annie. Claire.
Shey-Lee. Greta and Gen. and also Jacob and Antigone.
for their fantabulously fabulous ideas!—M.C.

Meredith Costain

For our beautiful girls Jade and Zoe—D.M.

Danielle McDonald

First American Edition 2016
Kane Miller, A Division of EDC Publishing

Text copyright © Meredith Costain, 2015
Illustrations copyright © Danielle McDonald, 2015

First published by Scholastic Australia, a division of Scholastic Australia Pty Limited in 2015.
This edition published under license from Scholastic Australia Pty Limited.

For information contact:
Kane Miller, A Division of EDC Publishing
PO Box 470663
Tulsa, OK 74147-0663
www.kanemiller.com
www.edcpub.com
www.usbornebooksandmore.com

Library of Congress Control Number: 2015954197

Printed and bound in the United States of America

4 5 6 7 8 9 10

ISBN: 978-1-61067-520-8

ELLA
Diaries

Double Dare You

Kane Miller
A DIVISION OF EDC PUBLISHING

Monday, after dinner

~~Dear Diary,~~

~~Hello Diary. My name's Ella and~~

~~Once upon a time there was~~
~~a girl called Ella. She lived~~

How are you supposed to start a diary? I've never had one before. Mom and Dad gave me this one for Christmas because

a) I like writing. I'm always writing stories and they love the poems I make up for their birthdays and other special days.

Inside of CARD

To Dad,

You're the best
My favorite relly
Even though
Your socks are smelly!

Happy Father's Day
with love from Ella x x x

b) They think I have a good imagination and they think writing something every day is a good way to "exercise" it.

c) I'm going into Grade 5 this year (starting tomorrow!) and Dad says Grade 5 was the best year of his life. He thinks I should write down all the things that happen each day so that when I'm an oldie like him I can look back and remember all the amazing and fun things I did over the year.

Well, that's what they think, anyway. My best friend, Zoe, has a diary, and she says that you can tell it all your secrets and stuff about how you feel, like when something makes you sad or angry.

I'm going to tell you absolutely everything, dearest Diary. But trust me—I'd never let anyone else get their hands on you . . . EVER.

TOP SECRET

So, here's my first secret, and only you will know. I'm, um . . . a little bit nervous about going back to school tomorrow. Phew, I said it! We've got a new teacher this year. What if we don't get along? Or she wants us to spend the whole year doing math problems or boring stuff like the names of rivers and capital cities?

The NiLe

PaRiS

I ♥ New York

$2 \times 2 =$ too boring!

Mr. Zugaro, my teacher last year, was amazing. We made up our own plays and acted them out and wrote all kinds of stories.

Amazing

Mr. Zugaro

He even showed us lots of different ways to write poems, which I love! ♥♥♥♥♥♥♥♥

And now I write them all the time. Here, in my room—not just for school. I guess you could call me a **secret scribbler.**

Oops! My little sister, Olivia, just came in but I managed to hide you under my pillow just in time. When it comes to people I don't want reading my diary, Olivia is at the top of my list.

LiST of <u>BANNED</u> people:

1. OLIVia →
2. <u>Mom</u>
3. Dad
4. ←Max
5. ~~Peach~~

TOP SECRET!

KEEP OUT!

Tuesday, straight after school

Hi, Diary, (hope you didn't miss me)

Eek! Today was the worst day of my life.
I am still shaking, see! It should have been
a really good day. Even though it
can be scary, there's something
really special about the first day
of school. I love the
smell of new books
and pencils and seeing
all my friends again and
everyone's always happy and
smiley after weeks and weeks
of summer vacation.

New
Pencil
Smell

Plus I was really excited because our new teacher, Ms. Weiss, has what Nanna Kate calls "personal style." Her outfit was TRULY inspired.

MS. WEISS

GLOSSY black HAIR

Hot-PINK flower

Matching PINK lipstick

BRIGHT-red dress

Hand-MADE Flowers

Sparkly tights

SUPER-Stylish sandals

Nanna Kate's always telling me I have great "personal style" as well. I like trying out different combinations of clothes too. Like

(pretty AND practical)

and

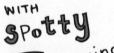

(sooo super stylish).

PLUS—and this is the best bit—Ms. Weiss is really into creative writing too!!! I can tell we are going to get along just fine.

As soon as the first bell went, all the kids in my new class lined up outside our room. Some of my old **year 4** FRIENDS

were there, like

And there were some new kids from the other classes as well. When Mr. Zugaro told us they were going to mix everyone up, I was really worried that they might split up Zoe and me. Zoe's been my Best Friend since Forever.

THINGS ZOE AND I LIKE DOING TOGETHER

* Swapping secrets
* Sleepovers (no
brothers—big OR little—allowed!)
* Music and dancing
(especially when we invent our own moves)
* Decorating cupcakes
* Designing stylish
outfit combos

But it was OK. We were safe. Mr. Zugaro
showed us the list with our names on it.
Zoe and I were definitely in the same class.

So far, everything was perfect.

So I wasn't expecting everything to go so
horribly wrong.

Zoe didn't turn up. Not even when Ms.
Weiss unlocked the door and we all started
finding tables to sit at. This is really
important because everyone knows that
the table you choose on the first day will
become your table for the WHOLE YEAR.

Unless there are what my Nanna Kate calls

UNFORESEEN
CIRCUMSTANCES.

1 Like a fridge falling out of an airplane, then dropping down through the roof into your classroom and smashing your table into smithereens.

2 Or a herd of angry elephants picking up your table with their trunks and hurling it out the window as they rampage past.

I'm pretty sure either of these things happening would mean you could move to a different table. But just in case they didn't I figured it would be wise to choose carefully the ~~minute~~ nanosecond we entered the classroom.

So I grabbed a table near the window (my favorite place to sit)

THINGS I LIKE TO LOOK AT OUT THE WINDOW

 trees

 birds

 trees with birds in them

 praying mantises

and waited for Zoe to arrive.

And waited.

And waited.

And waited.

No Zoe.

By now everyone else in the room had paired up. Maryam was sitting next to Sofie. Peter was sitting next to Raf. Even Cordelia, who usually prefers her own space, was sitting next to someone!

Everyone had a friend to sit next to, except me.

Some of the kids who'd come from the other classes were staring and whispering about me, sitting all alone at my table. I knew just what they were thinking. That girl doesn't have any friends. That girl is a BIG LOSER.

Still no Zoe.

Ms. Weiss asked us all to "settle down, please" then started calling out the names on the roll. She was just up to Sofie's name when I saw the handle turning on the classroom door.

Zoe! I thought.

creak

At last!

BiG LoSer

The door opened and a girl strolled into the room. Only it wasn't Zoe.

It was Peach.

Peach Parker. What was she doing in here?
Remember that list I told you about? The
one with Zoe's and my name on it? Well,
Peach's name *wasn't* on it. I remember doing
a happy dance in my head when I realized I
wouldn't have to share a classroom with her
anymore. Which means she wouldn't be able
to ~~copy ever~~ ever again.

Ms. Weiss welcomed her. She didn't ask her why she'd suddenly turned up late to a class she wasn't even supposed to be in. She just asked Peach to find a seat quickly so we could get started.

Peach looked over to where Prinny and Jade, her two best friends, sat waving like maniacs at her. But there was no room at their table of course. There was only one spare seat in the whole room, and we already know where that was, don't we?

Next to me.

I frantically piled all my books and pencil cases and project folders on the table in front of the empty chair so there was no room left for anyone else. Not even a very small dog that might have accidentally wandered into the room which would be excellent because apart from praying mantises, dogs are my favorite animal. If Zoe wasn't ever coming back, I would be very happy to share my table with a dog. Even Bob, our golden retriever, who is VERY large. And very licky.

Woof!

But it was no use. Ms. Weiss told Peach to sit at my table anyway.

The next bit is too painful and horrible and icky for me to write about right now. It's going to have to wait until tomorrow. Or maybe next year. Or maybe even next century.

Wednesday morning, before school

Good Bad morning, Diary,

I woke up really early and now I can't get back to sleep. I don't really want to go back to sleep anyway in case I have another bad dream.

In my dream I was being chased by a

GIANT piece of FRUIT.

It had long blond hair and big blue eyes
and it chased me right up to the edge of
a cliff. If I go back to sleep, it might chase
me over the top until I

f
a
l
l

into the swamp at the bottom of the
cliff and get all mashed up and eaten by
swamp monsters.

So I'm going to write about what happened yesterday instead.

WARNING: If you don't like horror stories, STOP READING NOW.

So Peach and I were both sitting at the table, as far away from each other as we could get. Peach kept turning around to make faces at her friends whenever Ms. Weiss was writing something on the board, and I kept looking out the window, in the hope that one of

CRASH

the planes flying overhead might drop a fridge on our table. Then Ms. Weiss would have to move us after all.

Only none of that happened. The planes kept flying right on by, no fridges fell out, and our table stayed exactly where it was.

Peach didn't say ONE WORD to me for the entire morning. Not even when Ms. Weiss gave us a project to do in pairs. I can't believe it. Ms. Weiss is expecting me to do a project about Adventures in Ancient Lands with Peach!!!! She obviously doesn't know anything about WHAT HAPPENED LAST YEAR.

Instead, Peach took out her perfect pencil case* and Deluxe Set of gel and glitter pens** and started writing down her ideas in her ultra-neat handwriting. All hunched over with her arm hooked around her folder of course, so I couldn't see what she was writing. AS IF I CARE!

PeRfecT

* Which is EXACTLY like the one I wanted Mom to get me for Christmas, except she didn't, even though I dropped some VERY big hints and left the STATIONERY"R"US catalog lying around in very conspicuous

places. Like inside her
cereal bowl.

** Another very important item on my
gift wish list.

When the bell went for recess, Peach, Prinny
and Jade went out to the playground, arm
in arm. They kept looking over at me while
I was playing downball with Maryam and
Sofie and whispering and giggling, like they
knew something I didn't know. But I just
ignored them, and went right on playing

DOWNBall ♥

(It's like four square
except you can also use
your head and your feet.)

I played downball at lunchtime too, along
with most of the other kids in our class.
I kept hoping Zoe would turn up but she
didn't. She still wasn't there when we went
back in after lunch either.

↓ Bleuchh! ←

But Peach was.

And she did her best to get me into
trouble with Ms. Weiss every chance she
could.

She waited till Ms. Weiss was writing on
the board again, then did a really big, loud,
stinky burp.

Ms. Weiss turned around with a shocked
look on her face and said, "Oooo, manners!"
Peach looked straight at me
and said, "Ewww. What did you
do *that* for?" as though I was
the one who'd burped! Then she
put her hand up and said, "Excuse
me, Ms. Weiss, would you like me to go to
the office and get the air freshener?"

Ms. Weiss said, "That's really thoughtful of you, Peach, but I think we'll be fine for now." And then she added Peach's name to the STUDENT STARS section of the board, for being so helpful. She didn't say anything to me but I could tell by the look on her face that she definitely thought I'd done the burp.

Student Stars

Tom
Alice
Peach

Then later on Peach passed a note to Prinny and Ms. Weiss caught Prinny and Jade giggling over it. She asked them to read out what the note said. They made a big fuss at first about doing that, and then they read it aloud in REALLY ANNOYING voices.

Ms. Weiss is weird. She looks like a birthday cake.

Signed: Ella
PS Pass it on

Everyone turned around and stared at me. Peach was staring the hardest, like she was shocked that she was sitting next to someone who could write something like that.

Ms. Weiss looked straight at me and said (in a really quiet, sad, desolate* voice): "Did you write this, Ella?"

Sad

←--- Ms. Weiss

* The type of voice princesses use when their knights in shining armor have deserted them in high towers with no steps.

KnighT in SHINING ARMOR

I went as red as Ms. Weiss's dress. Then
I looked down at the table and shook my
head. "No, Ms. Weiss," I whispered.

But I don't think she believed me. Not after
the burp.

Ms. Weiss asked Prinny for the note. She
crumpled it up and threw it INto the trash.
She made a speech, to the whole class,
in a very serious voice about how it
was wrong to say mean things about
other people. Then she told us all to
work without speaking to anyone for
the next ten minutes. Ha! Like I'd want to
speak to Peach EVER AGAIN. 10 Minutes

NO TALKING

Why did Zoe have to be away today? If she'd been at school none of these horrible, ugly, detestable things would have happened.

Where is Zoe, anyway? I called her house yesterday afternoon but there was no answer. There still wasn't any answer when I tried again before bedtime. I hope her family hasn't been sucked up into a vortex or something. If they have I'll be stuck with Peach at my table forever.

My life is ruined. I've lost my best friend. And now lovely, stylish Ms. Weiss (who I was sure was going to be my favorite teacher) HATES me!

Reasons 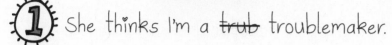 Ms. Weiss HATES ME

1. She thinks I'm a ~~trub~~ troublemaker.

2. She thinks I don't have any manners.

3. She thinks I'm a (smelly) burper.

4. She thinks I'm making fun of her style (which is so not fair, because I think she is the MOST stylish teacher I have ever had!).

AND it's ALL Peach PARKER'S FAULT!

Wednesday, after dinner

Dear amazing, wonderful, fabulous Diary,

Zoe is back!

I am sooo relieved. (Can you tell?) Zoe's family wasn't sucked up into a vortex after all! She was waiting in our special place in the playground when I arrived at school. Her nonna broke her hip early yesterday morning and Zoe's mom had to rush off to the country to look after

her. She took Zoe and her older brother, Will, with her. She said by the time they got home it was too late to call me.

Maybe if she had called I wouldn't have had so many bad dreams about fruit. ☹

I told Zoe all about how Ms. Weiss had made Peach sit next to me and how Peach had tricked Ms. Weiss into thinking I was a mean note-writing burper. Zoe said sorry about six times and I could tell she really meant it.

That's why she's my best friend. Then she said to fix things we needed to write a petition to Ms. Weiss with two aims:

Aim 1. Change Ms. Weiss's opinion of me from a negative one to a positive one.

Aim 2. Convince Ms. Weiss to let us sit together.

Just as she was telling me the second aim,
Ms. Weiss walked past us on her way to
the teachers' lounge. She was talking to Mr.
Zugaro so I'm pretty sure she didn't see
us. Her outfit today was even more stylish
than the one she was wearing yesterday.
I was dying to tell her how wonderful she
looked, but I didn't in case she thought I
was trying to make fun of her again.
AS IF I WOULD!!

Anyway, her tantalizing trendsetting outfit
gave me an idea for the petition.

Here's what we wrote:

Dear Ms. Weiss,

You are looking very lovely today. (In fact nothing at all like a birthday cake. I can't believe someone wrote that. Unless it was a really nice one, which ~~acksherty~~ actually when you think about it, most birthday cakes usually are.) We especially like the way you have teamed a bright-red bolero top with a green dress with purple swirls on it and a matching purple flower in your hair. We also like your earrings. ~~Did they cost a lot of money?~~*

It is very important that my best friend, Zoe, (who was away yesterday) and I sit together in class this year.

Bright
bolero
TOP
Purple
Swirls
Green
Dress

Here ARE the ReasoNs WHY

1. Zoe and I have been best friends since forever.

2. It isn't Zoe's fault that she missed out on the first day of school when important decisions like table choosing are made. She was having a family ~~emurjency~~ emergency.

3. Zoe has a medical ~~condishun~~ condition which means that if she doesn't sit next to a very close friend she will break out into an itchy rash. Which might be catching.

4. I have the same ~~condish~~ condition.

5. ~~If I have to sit next to Peach for even one more minute I will die.~~ **

Thank you for considering our request.

Yours truly,

Ella and Zoe

* Zoe made me take this bit out because she said her mom told her it is rude to ask people how much their things cost.

** Zoe made me take this bit out as well. She said we should only write things that are true. But this IS true!

I nearly did chicken out, but Zoe put her arm around me, and smiled at me in a very kind and SOLID way, and together we knocked  on the teachers' lounge door and asked for Ms. Weiss. We gave her the petition and she read it right there in the doorway in front of us, while all the other teachers nearly knocked her over as they rushed off to their classrooms. I was worried she might be cross (especially because there were so many spelling mistakes, and because of all the bruises she must be getting from all those rushing teachers) but when she finally stopped reading and looked up at us she didn't look cross.

She looked happy. I could tell she was happy because she was laughing. People only laugh when they're happy, right?

Then she told me I was a "sweetheart"
(Me!!!) and she didn't believe I was capable
of doing smelly burps when her back was
turned, even if other people tried to say I
did. (Which means maybe she doesn't hate
me after all. Phewww...)

And then she said of course Zoe and I could
sit together and she would find somewhere
else for Peach to sit. She said there'd been
last minute changes to class numbers so
there hadn't been enough chairs and tables
in the room, but it had all been fixed up
now, and to hurry along to our classroom
because the bell was about to ring.

And here's the best bit. When we went into our classroom, there was a new table at the front of the room, right in front of Ms. Weiss's desk.

And guess who Ms. Weiss told to sit at that table?

HINT: Their name rhymes with

"BEACH."

Thursday, after school

Hey there, Diary,

Peach hasn't spoken to me since Ms. Weiss asked her to sit at the new table. You would think this would be a good thing and mostly it is, but it also makes me a bit nervous and twitchy, in case she is planning something to get me back.

So I wrote this haiku about her.

The volcano sits
Its sides shaking and heaving
waiting to erupt

Mr. Zugaro taught us how to write haiku last year. Haiku are Japanese poems about nature. They have three lines and each line has to have five or seven sillybubbles* in it.

* I think that's what they're called.

Friday, before lights-out

Hey, Diary-doo,

Nanna Kate is here looking after Olivia and Max and me because Mom and Dad have gone to the movies. They are probably going to sit really close to each other in the back row and hold hands. They might even KISS each other. Ewwwwww. But I am HAPPY, HAPPY, HAPPY because Nanna Kate and I spent TWO WHOLE HOURS going through my closet trying out different outfit combinations. She even let me stay up a whole hour later than I normally do.

OUTFIT #1

SPARKLY S·C·A·R·F

stripy top

E

MOM's Necklace

ZIP-UP BOOTS

OUTFIT #2

cap

favorite T-shirt

BANGLES

Tartan skirt

LONG STRIPY SOCKS

Nanna Kate is the BEST Nanna in the WHOLE WILD WORLD.

Good night
Sleep tight
Don't let
Your mean friends bite.

OUTFIT 3

tiara

and

PARty DRESS

with

Gum boots

Saturday night, just before dinner

Hello again, Diary,

Mom took me to Parkfields Shoppingtown today to buy me some new sneakers for the cross-country event that's coming up soon. I found some purple ones with pink sparkles across the toes. They were so AMAZINGLY ATTRACTIVE I had to wear them out of the store.

sparkles pink

Cordelia was in the shoe store buying sneakers too. Hers were OK, but not as spectacularly, splendidly sensational as mine.✳

The only bad thing about the day was that Olivia and Max came too, and they spent all their time whining and bugging Mom to buy them ice cream when I'd rather have been looking at FASHION. And guess where Max's ice cream ended up?

Yep. You got it.

ALL OVER my beautiful new shoes. Little brothers and sisters are SOOO embarrassing!

* As you have probably noticed by now, I like using words that start with the same sound.

Sunday morning, just before lunch

Bob dug his way out under the front fence again and bounced up at Mr. Supramaniam when he went past in his motorized wheelchair. Mr. Supramaniam got a fright and crashed his wheelchair into our next-door neighbor's fence. And now he is in BIG TROUBLE. (Bob, not Mr. Supramaniam. Although I don't think our next-door neighbor is very happy about what Mr. Supramaniam did to his fence.)

Have to go now, Mom wants me to set the table for lunch!

Monday, straight after school

Dear Diary,

Roses are red
Praying mantises are green
Precious Peach Parker
Makes me want to SCREAM!

That is all.

Tuesday, after school

G'day, G'Diary,

It's official. There's a new craze at school. Last year it was making loom bands. Everyone (well, except for Cordelia, who's not really into that kind of stuff) sat around in the playground with plastic looms and a rainbow of rubber bands and made friendship bracelets for each other. Peach and Prinny and Jade had so many bracelets it gives me a headache just thinking about how big a number that must be.

13362578889947

The year before that it was Chinese jump rope, or French skipping—which is what my Nanna Kate used to call it when she was at school about nine hundred years ago. Zoe and Peach* and I used to play it every lunchtime. We chanted rhymes while we were skipping. This one was my favorite:

> Henry, Henry (or whoever you
> thought was annoying)
> Sitting on a pin
> How many inches did the pin go in?
> One, two, three, four.

Of course you know whose name I would put in the first line now, don't you? ☺

* This was when Peach and I were still best friends, before the mean, terrible, nasty, awful, horrible, dreadful, shocking thing she did to me at the start of last year, which I will never ever EVER forgive her for. Ever.

Anyway, the new craze this year is downball. As soon as the bell goes for recess or lunch there's a big stampede to grab one of the downball courts. There are only six courts so there are always lines of kids waiting for the first four players to go out so they can get into a game.

DownBall

Today Zoe and I played Peter and Raf.

Zoe was playing like a star, serving up some really hot balls and smashing them around the court. She even threw in a few footsies. Then Peter did a low return that skimmed across the ground. Zoe raced for it but she was too late. The ball double-bounced in her square and she was out. I moved up to King and Sofie went to Dunce.

We stayed in for ages. I could see the kids waiting in line getting more and more fidgety, waiting for their chance to play. Finally Peter hit a terrible shot and went out, which meant he had to go right to the end of the line.

I stayed in though, for the whole of recess. I even did a header!

My Header

Downball is the best. You don't have to sit around in little groups all the time, worrying about what people might be saying or thinking about you in other little groups. You get to move around really fast all over the court. I love it.

In fact, I love it so much I made up this poem about it.

Playing downball is good fun
Always keeps you on the run
Makes you want to sing and shout
Just make sure you don't go out!

Wednesday, before bedtime

Hey there, Diary,

I CANNOT believe what happened at school today.

We were all working on our Adventures in Ancient Lands projects. Zoe and I are doing Ancient Egypt. We've invented a character called Professor Violet Higginbottom who discovers a secret chamber in a pyramid that has been buried for centuries under the sands of the Egyptian desert. Inside the chamber is the mummified body of an Egyptian pharaoh. And lots of treasure, and those little stone jars they keep all the guts in. And slaves to look after them in the next life, and mummified cats. We're even drawing a map showing the secret passageways inside the pyramid.

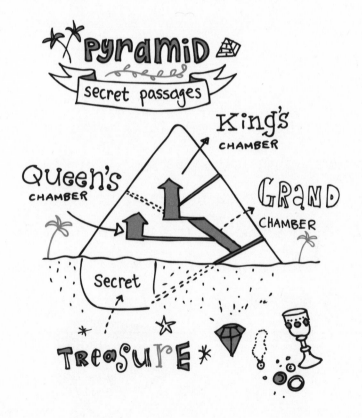

Ms. Weiss said three people from the class could give a report on how their projects were going. Ms. Weiss chose Peter first. He and Raf are writing an adventure starring some of the Greek gods. Then she chose Daisy, who's writing about Ancient China with Grace.

She looked over at our table and I was sure she was going to choose me. Only Peach's hand shot up really high and she said (in that whiny voice she uses when she wants to suck up to teachers): "Please, Ms. Weiss, can Prinny, Jade and I go next? We're just sooo excited about our project."

PLEASE

So annoying!!

Bleuchhh. I was SURE Ms. Weiss would roll her eyes around in her head like I was doing. But instead she said, "Yes, of course, Peach. We'd love to hear all about it, wouldn't we, class?" And then before everyone could call out "Nooooooooooooooo!" she awarded Peach another Student Star for being so refreshingly "Super Enthusiastic."

Bleuchhh to the power of ten trillion!!! So Peach stood up and said her group's project was about Ancient Egypt.

Uh-oh, I thought. Surely she's not going to do it again . . .

And then she said they're writing about an explorer who finds a pyramid no one has ever seen before and inside the pyramid is . . .

You know what's coming next, don't you?

Inside the pyramid is a secret chamber with the mummy of a "lost" pharaoh in it. Plus all the other things like the treasure and the jars for guts and the slaves and even the mummified cat we're putting inside our secret chamber.

Zoe and I looked at each other with our mouths hanging wide open while Ms. Weiss congratulated Peach's team for coming up

with such an "original idea" and
awarded them all a Student Star.  **STUdenT StaR**

Peach looked over at our table and
gave us both this really **Fake Smile**.
Then she sat down again and
started coloring something
in with a yellow marker.
Probably a map of the secret
passageways leading to the secret chambers
inside the secret pyramid she copied off us.

Now what are we supposed to do? If we
keep going with our project Ms. Weiss will
think we copied Peach's idea. But if I tell
Ms. Weiss that Peach copied our idea (I

don't know exactly how she did it yet, but she definitely did) then Peach will just deny it and everything will end up in a big mess, JUST LIKE IT DID LAST TIME*. Zoe and I are going to have to come up with a whole new idea for our project. Why couldn't Peach just stay in the class she was supposed to be in this year?

* I wonder if Peach realizes she doesn't need to copy things I write because she's actually a good writer herself. Oops! I just gave away part of the terrible, horrible, bad thing she did. So I might as well tell you what happened.

Last year we both
decided to enter a
writing competition. I had this
brilliant idea for a mystery
story with a really cool ending.
I told Peach all about it at recess one day.
But when the results of the competition
came out, Peach's story
won first prize—and it
was almost exactly the
same as mine! I tried to
tell people that Peach had copied my ideas,
but she just said I'd copied hers, and I
was trying to spread fibs about her. Total
betrayal! And that's why we're not best
friends anymore.

Thursday morning, before school

I had really bad dreams again last night. This time, a volcano was erupting. And big pieces of fruit were shooting out of the top and running down the sides. I tried to run away but it was like my legs were moving through a mass of marshmallow, and I got drenched in icky, sticky sliced fruit.

Thursday, after school

Dearest Diary,

The good news
We played downball again today. As soon as
the bell went, Zoe and I ran for the courts
to make sure we got a game. And we did.
(Sadly, it all goes

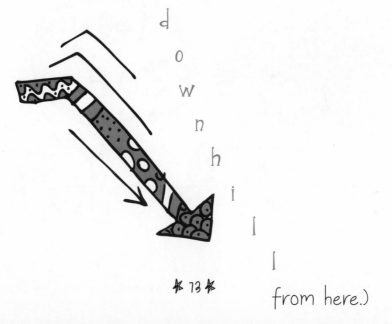

d
o
w
n
h
i
l
l

from here.)

The bad news

Peach and her friends were in line. They kept calling out silly things like "El-la's a smel-la" and "Don't be so toe-y, Zoe-y" so we'd mis-hit the ball and go out. My face went a bit red when Peach called me "a smel-la," but I just ignored her and kept playing.

The worse news

Then Sofie did a really sneaky shot and I hit it out of the court. I was out, so off I went to the back of the line, just behind Daisy.

The ~~worser worserer~~ even worse news

The line of bored people standing around waiting to play seemed much shorter than when we first started playing. Why? I hear you asking. I did too:

Me: What happened to the kids waiting to play? Half of them are missing.
Daisy (laughing nervously): They . . . er . . . went with Peach.

Me (suspiciously): Went
with Peach where?
Daisy (pointing to the big
pepper tree near the fence): Over there.
Me: And this was because . . .?
Daisy (more nervous laughter): Um . . . it
was right after she said, "Come on, this is a
BABIES' GAME for LOSERS. We're out of here."
Me (looking over at people **I THOUGHT
WERE MY FRIENDS** laughing and joking
with Peach): Oh.

But secretly I was thinking,
Good. I hope they go there next
lunchtime too. I don't want to
play downball with Precious

PEPPER tree

Princess Peach Parker AND ANYONE ELSE WHO WANTS TO HANG OUT WITH HER anyway.

YAY!

No Peach = DOWN BaLL

Friday, just before dinner

Dear Diary,

Today at school Ms. Weir

Sorry about that. Olivia just came into my room and interrupted me, so I had to hide you under my pillow. I don't think she saw you though . . .

Olivia always wants to borrow my stuff.
I tell her to get her own stuff and she
goes whining off to Mom about it, saying
how mean I am. And then Mom says (in
that really serious "Mom" voice she puts
on sometimes): "Now, Ella, you know how
important it is to share your things with
other people. Especially someone as sweet
and kind as your darling little sister."

Bleuchhh.

How come Olivia never has to
share her stuff with me? Then
again, who would want to borrow her stuff
anyway? All her things are plain, plain, plain.

sweet
(olivia)

She would never think of this masterpiece:

Feather
BOA

Tiger-
PRINT
DRESS

Pink glitter shoes

She has absolutely NO sense of personal style at all.

Mom's calling me to come and set the table so I have to stop now. We're having spag bol— My Favorite. `Yum!`

I'll write more after dinner.

Friday, just after dinner

Sorry, dearest Diary, I'm back.

Something really weird happened at school today. Ms. Weiss was in the middle of telling us about how solids, liquids and gases behave when Georgia suddenly stood up and started doing the CHICKEN DANCE. Right in the middle of the classroom! She was flapping her arms and making little beak shapes with her hands and wiggling up and down. She even did a few chicken noises. And then she sat down again, looking straight ahead as though nothing had happened.

Of course everyone started laughing and
talking about what we'd just seen, and Ollie
and Zac started making B-Burrrkkkk!
chicken noises of their own. But then Ms.
Weiss called for quiet and everyone settled
down again.

Ms. Weiss just smiled at Georgia, and said she hoped she was feeling better soon, and that whatever it was she had wasn't catching. Then she went back to telling us what happens to liquids and gases when you heat them. Everyone kept waiting for Georgia to do the CHICKEN DANCE again, but she didn't. She didn't even make any chicken noises.

Like I said. Weird.

Monday, after school

Greetings, O most excellent Diary of mine.

Guess what happened today. Poppy went up to Jacob Curry (this really popular guy in Grade 6 who's captain of all the sports teams) and TALKED TO HIM. Poppy! She's the quietest, shyest girl in our grade. And then at lunchtime, her best friend Chloe started up a conga line of dancers (including Mr. Bing and Ms. Sneddon, who were both on lunch duty at the time) that snaked all around the playground.

Ms. Sneddon

Cha-cha-cha

MR.
Bing

Tuesday, after dinner

Hey, Diary,

I'm supposed to be doing my homework but there is so much more important stuff to write about! Today Mr. Martini, the principal, found a plastic fake vomit on the windshield of his car. Peter said he saw him picking it up with a tissue (in case it was real) and throwing it into the bushes.

I'm glad it was fake vomit and not a real one. Even thinking about real vomit makes me feel sick, ever since I stepped in a pool of dog vomit after Bob accidentally got locked in the pantry and chowed his way through six packets of Hot'n'Spicy dry noodles and three packets of instant cupcake mix (with strawberry icing).

Then later, during math, this happened:

Alysha (squirming around in her chair): Excuse me, Ms. Weiss.

Ms. Weiss: Yes, Alysha.

Alysha: I'm BUSTING. Can I go to the bathroom, please?

Ms. Weiss (looking concerned):
Yes, of course you can.
FIVE MINUTES LATER. . .
Alysha (waving hand in the
air): Excuse me, Ms. Weiss.
Ms. Weiss: Yes, Alysha.
Alysha (innocently): I'm busting AGAIN.
Can I go to the bathroom, please?
Ms. Weiss (wrinkling her forehead in that
way teachers do when they think someone
is trying to pull a swifty, but they're not
100% sure): I don't think so, Alysha. You've
just been. Wait till recess, please.
FIVE MINUTES LATER . . .
Alysha (waving hand in the air): Excuse me,
Ms. Weiss.

Ms. Weiss (smiling thinly): Yes, Alysha.

Alysha (even more innocently): I'm STILL busting. Can I go to the bathroom, please?

Ms. Weiss: No.

And this kept happening every five minutes until the bell went. Alysha NEVER does stuff like that!

OK, will stop now and do my math homework. ☹ ☹ ☹

No . . . wait! I feel a poem coming!

> Math homework
> So boring that I'm snoring
> Trying . . . sighing . . . crying
> Makes me want to VOMIT!!!

Wednesday, just before bedtime

Dearest, darlingest Diary,

I've been waiting all day to tell you this,
but now I'm not sure that I can, in case it
makes me too sad . . . ☹ Oh well, here goes.

It's about our downball games. The line of
people waiting to play is getting shorter
and shorter each day. Today, when I hit
another shot out and had to go to the
back of the line, there were only three kids
in front of me. I heard all this laughing
coming from over near the pepper tree, and
surprise, surprise, Peach was there, with her

little friends. But also lots of other kids from our class . . . like Alysha and Lily, and Chloe and Poppy . . . sitting in a big circle. Those girls don't even LIKE Peach.

Then, suddenly, Lily stood up and everyone started clapping and chanting:

"Do it! Do it!" **Do it.** :Do it!:

Do it!

DO IT!

Lily started walking towards the downball courts. I thought she was going to join the line but she went right past me to the trash, which was full to the top with stinky lunch leftovers and banana peels. Then Lily bent over and put her face right up close to the trash.

"Do it! Do it!" chanted the crowd.

Lily gave the trash can a big sloppy kiss. The kids under the tree stopped chanting "Do it!" and started cheering instead.

"Yuck!" squealed Lily. "That was disgusting."
Then she laughed so much I thought her head
was going to fall off.

And then I noticed something else. I was the
only one left in the line. All the others had
gone to join Peach.

☹☹☹☹☹☹☹

Thursday, straight after school

I have to write about what happened today before I BURST!!

When Zoe and I ran over to the downball courts at lunchtime, we were the only ones there. Everyone else was in a big circle under the pepper tree, laughing and joking. Even Peter and Raf!

We played two square for a while but it wasn't any fun without the others. We kept stopping and looking over at their silly circle, wondering what they were all doing.

♥Things they MIGHT BE DOinG IN THE CircLe

AND reasons WHY OR WHY NOT

	WHY	WHY NOT
1. Playing Murder in the Dark	It's played in a circle	It wasn't dark
2. Playing Drop the Hanky	It's played in a circle	It's a babies' game
3. Playing Duck, Duck, Goose	It's played in a circle	It's an even babier game

There was only one way to find out.
We were going to have to
join them. So we walked
over to the pepper tree.
I made Zoe walk first in
case Peach had booby-
trapped the path.

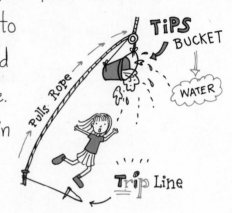

TIPS
BUCKET
WATER
Pulls Rope
Trip Line

As we got closer to the circle we noticed
Peach was actually sitting just outside it,
on a kind of throne made out of small logs
and cushions. Maybe Peach thinks she really
is a princess. She was even wearing a
crown. (Though it looked just like the cheap,
tinny one Olivia wears when she's playing
dress up with her friend Matilda.)

CHEAP tinny CROWN

Cushion THRONE

Peach started being all fakey nice when she saw us standing on the edge of her circle. She reached over and tapped Poppy lightly on the arm, then asked her to move over so we could join in the fun.

And then I noticed something else sitting right in the middle of the circle.

A
LARGE
BLACK
SHOE

We squeezed in between Poppy and Chloe.
Everyone was staring at the shoe, like
it had magical powers or was about to
turn into a boy wizard or a fire-breathing
dragon.

Then Poppy asked Peach if she could have
a turn spinning the shoe. But Peach said
only Prinny and Jade—The Official Keepers
of the Shoe—were allowed to do that. Prinny
shuffled across into the center of the circle

and picked up the shoe. She held it a few inches above the ground, then gave it a fast flick with her fingers so that it spun around a few times. It was pretty boring. No flames shot out of it and no one got turned into a frog. Or even a praying mantis. Everyone started calling out, "It's landed on Zoe!"

But then I got it. The toe of the shoe was *pointing* at Zoe. She'd been CHOSEN by the shoe and now something was going to happen to her.

zoe

The Chosen ONE

Peach leaned back on her throne and smiled like a snake*. Then she said:

The shoe has landed
Fair and square
And now you have to
Do a dare.

* I'm not 100% sure that snakes can actually smile, but if they could, they'd look like Peach on her throne.

Aha! So it's a DARING game. Suddenly it all made sense. I was so proud when Zoe smiled back and said, "Bring it on."

Zoe's really brave like that. But she probably hadn't realized when she said it that the dares Peach gives out are mostly very silly or embarrassing for the person doing them.

Super zoe

She might change her mind about being brave if she finds out she has to do the budgie dance** in class or kiss the part of Mr. Martini's windshield that the fake (or—EWWW!—real, we never actually found out) vomit was stuck to.

So anyway, after Zoe said to bring it on, Peach said, "OK, here's what you have to do . . ."

Sorry, Diary, have to go. Mom's calling me!

** The budgie dance is closely related to the chicken dance, only the steps are based on the movements of budgies rather than chickens. Not many people know the steps to this one because Olivia and I made it up in our family room one day, before she became so annoying.

Budgie DANCE.

Friday, after school

Hey there, Diary-O,

Zoe is still really upset. I raided my emergency piggy bank—the one with the sign on it that says:

KEEP OUT

ONLY to be opened in case of CALAMITOUS catastrophe.

THIS MEANS **YOU**

I bought as many of her favorite chocolate bars as I could from the store on the corner but she says she's never going back to school because she won't be able to face anyone on the sports committee EVER AGAIN.

Here's what happened.

We always have a special sports assembly on Friday mornings where all the team captains give their sports reports. Zoe is captain of the girls' swim team for our grade and she had her speech all prepared.

But Zoe's dare was that she had to take out all the people's names, or the names of events, in her speech and replace them with the words "Grandma's undies." So this is what her speech sounded like:

Good morning, Grandma's undies, my name is Grandma's undies and today I am giving you the report about Grandma's undies.

(Everyone was already laughing by this stage but Zoe kept reading, even though her face was as red as the banner on the wall behind her.)

Grandma's undies

Last Wednesday, we held the tryouts for Grandma's undies in the Grandma's undies Memorial Swimming Pool. Twenty-six students from all grade levels competed in the following events—Grandma's undies. Grandma's undies. Grandma's undies. and finally. Grandma's undies—in the hope of gaining a place on the team.

The following students were chosen to represent us: Grandma's undies. Grandma's undies. Grandma's undies. Grandma's undies—and as an alternate this year—Grandma's undies.

By this time all the students in the hall were howling with laughter※ and some of the Grade 4

boys had fallen off their
chairs and were rolling
around on the floor.

Even Mr. Martini was
making these strangled,
snorting noises, like he was
trying not to laugh but
couldn't hold it in anymore.

* Howling with laughter is what my Nanna
Kate says is the best way to describe the
way people laugh when they're laughing really
hard, but it sounds like something a wolf
would do and I'm not 100% sure that wolves
can actually laugh.

Anyway, after that last bit Zoe had to stop reading her report because she said she was too ~~embariss~~ ~~embarruss~~ embarrassed to keep on going. The only way I could cheer her up was by agreeing to play Spin the Shoe again. If it landed on me, I promised CROSS MY *heart* Hope to DIE that I would do the dare Peach said I had to and not even THINK about backing out of it. Because Zoe thinks that any dare Peach sets for me is going to be a trillion times worse than the Grandma's Undies one.

This could all go REALLY, REALLY badly.
But it's what best friends do, isn't it?
They agree to do difficult things for their

friends even though it might mean maximum embarrassment to the power of ~~ten~~ one thousand for them.

BUT (HoRRoR of horrors to the power of gatrillion) now I have to wait until Monday to find out what Peach's dare is going to be!!!!!

Saturday, before lunch

I'm starting to get really twitchy about the
dare Peach is going to give me.
What if she . . .

Saturday, after lunch

No, she wouldn't do that. Would she???

Saturday, before dinner

Or maybe she's going to
make me . . .

Saturday, after dinner

I can't bear the suspense anymore. I wish Monday would hurry up and come.

Sunday, first thing

NO, I DON'T!!!!!

Sunday, before bed

I'm wondering if I draw spots on my tummy with a red marker I'd be able to convince Mom that I had Occhilupo's disease✳ which has an itchy red rash that is HIGHLY contagious (that means you can catch it

Occhilupo's
Disease

easily from people who already have it)
and therefore I won't be able to go to
school tomorrow. But that would mean
breaking my promise to Zoe and I don't
want to do that.

* This disease doesn't actually exist but
it sounds like it might, doesn't it? Mom
isn't a nurse or a doctor or anything so
how would she know that I just made it up

after seeing the name on the back of one
of Dad's old surfing magazines from the
year 10,000 BC.

Monday, before bedtime

So at lunchtime today Zoe and I took a
couple of deep breaths, linked arms, and
went back to the circle of kids under the
pepper tree. (As you can probably tell
by now, I decided NOT to pretend I had
Occhilupo's disease
after all and went to
school to face Peach's
dare instead.)
When we got there

Princess Peach was sitting on her throne again, only this time she was wearing a bigger, tinnier crown  with even more fake jewels on it. YAWN. Doesn't she know ANYTHING about regal style??? Obviously NOT.

Prinny and Jade were still the only ones allowed to spin the shoe. It's so obvious that they're totally rigging where it lands. Surely anyone with even a tiny brain in their head knows that. Peach was still the only one who was allowed to give out the dares.

BIGGER CROWN

It was Jade's turn to spin the shoe. And surprise, surprise, guess who it landed on.

HINT: Their name rhymes with "Umbrella."

I took a deep breath and looked straight at Peach. And then I asked her what my dare was.

Peach gave me another one of her snake smiles and said, "You know Cordelia, who is in our class?"

And I said, "Yes, of course I know Cordelia. Everyone knows Cordelia."

But the whole time I was saying that I was worrying about what Peach was going to dare me to do. Because Cordelia is this really sweet, lovely girl but she's not like anyone else in my year. Most kids go all weird if their best friend is away for even one day (like I did!) but she's quite happy hanging out by herself. She has this great toy furry animal collection and sometimes she brings some of the animals to school and talks to them like they're her friends.

I looked across the playground to the library steps where Cordelia usually spends recess and lunchtimes. She was sitting there reading a book, with Mr. Wombat snuggled up on her lap. Everyone knows Mr. Wombat is her favorite furry toy.

And then Peach said, "I dare you to kidnap Mr. Wombat from Cordelia when she's not looking and hide him somewhere she can't find him."

I quickly looked at Zoe, who was waiting for me to keep my promise to her and accept the dare. And then I looked over at Cordelia

again, sitting all alone on the
library steps. Mr. Wombat was
the only true friend she had in
the whole world.

Peach could see I was wavering about what
to do. "OK," she said, her eyes going all
snaky again. "**DOUBLE DARE YOU**."
Double dares are really hard to refuse. If
you back down from a double dare at our
school, it means you're chicken. No one likes
other kids to think they're chicken.
Plus Zoe was counting on me as well.
It would be super-duper easy for
me to get Mr. Wombat away from Cordelia
without her knowing. I even knew about

sixty hiding places that she'd
never think of looking for him
in. Zoe would be happy again
and no one would think I was
chicken for backing out of a
double dare.

#13 plant pot

But then I thought about
how Cordelia was going to
feel trying to get to sleep
that night without her best friend to talk

#29 behind bush

to. And Zoe already has lots
of other friends, even if she
didn't want
to be mine
any more.

#3 in a toy truck

#46 on a bookshelf

I stood up and went over to where Peach was sitting on her throne.

"Yeah?" I said, looking down at her. "Well, I don't care if you *triple dare* me, I'm not going to do it. Cordelia loves Mr. Wombat and I'm not going to take him away from her."

Then I heard all these clapping sounds. Only this time it wasn't the other kids slow clapping while they chanted, "Do it! Do it!"

This time they were just clapping for me
for standing up to Peach and her silly dares.

Princess Peach stuck her nose in the air.
"Come on," she said to Prinny and Jade.
"Let's go. I'm bored with this game now
anyway." And they stomped off.

Everyone in the circle just sat there looking
at each other, wondering what to do next.

Then two boys ran past, chasing a
basketball that had bounced off the court
they were playing on. It gave me a really
good idea.

I pointed to the rest of the kids on the
basketball court, running up and down
and shooting baskets. "Who wants to play
basketball?" I asked.
"Me!" yelled all the kids in the
circle. Including Zoe.

Yay

So that's what we all did. Who knows?
Maybe we'll even start a new craze!

Good night, dear Diary.

PS (one week later)

Oh yeah. Remember those projects we were doing? About Adventures in Ancient Lands? Well, the weirdest thing happened. Cordelia's project partner, Joybelle, ended up getting chicken pox (she had bright-red spots all over her face and tummy just like people who have Occhilupo's disease would get if it was actually a real disease and not just one I made up) and so Ms. Weiss asked her to work with me and Zoe instead.

ReAL SPOTS

And GUESS WHAT!!

You never will (and I'm tired and want to go to sleep now) so I'll just tell you.

It turns out Cordelia (who reads A LOT of books) knows all this AMAZING stuff about an ancient tribe of warrior women called the Samartians, who rode around on horseback having adventures and fighting battles. So we changed our project to be about that.

Samartians
Warrior WOMEN

And GUESS WHAT ELSE!!!

Ms. Weiss said our topic was so interesting and original she gave us special bonus points, and our team project WON!!

Guess who wasn't very happy about that????

HINT: Her name rhymes with "leech."

Grrrr......

Leech

CLASS 5 W

Adventures in Ancient Lands Project

- -

BEST TEAM

ELLA, ZOE and CORDELIA

- -

Ms E. Weiss

MS. E. WEISS

PPS (two weeks later)

And remember how I said basketball might become our new craze?

Well, I must have psychic powers or something, because **IT DID!!!** Only we call it B-Ball.

Zoe and I (and just about everyone else in our class, except for You Know Who x 3) race over to the B-Ball courts as soon as the bell rings. Zoe and Peter are the best shooters and Cordelia is the referee (she learned the rules from a book in the library). And Mr. Wombat is our mascot! He sits on the sidelines and watches every game. Sometimes he even helps out Cordelia with difficult refereeing decisions.

I love B-Ball so much I wrote this song about it.

B-Ball, B-Ball
You're the best
Play it when
You're feeling stressed
Shooting baskets
All day long
Join me in
My B-Ball song!

B-Ball 4 EVER. YEAH!!!!

Make your own diary!
Put a photo of yourself in the frame
below and write your name in the oval!

Diaries

Top 10 things you LOVE to do:

 1

 2

 3

 4

 5

 6

 7

 8

 9

10

Write your own haiku!

Haiku are Japanese poems about nature. They have three lines and each line has to have five or seven syllables in it.

Draw the funkiest fashion you can imagine!

SNEAK
PEEK

ELLA

Diaries

Ballet
Backflip

Saturday, before dinner

Dear Diary,

You will never ever EVER believe what happened today!

I was at ballet class like I normally am every Saturday morning. My ballet class is held at:

(which is just a fancy French way of saying Mrs. Fry's ballet school. Except, actually, the school isn't very fancy at all).

The main reason for this is because ballet is held in our local scout hall. Which means when we're not there, the scouts are. Which is a VERY BAD THING.

Reasons why sharing YOUR SPACE with SCOUTS is BAD:

① The scouts are (mostly) boys.

② The boys often SMELL BAD. (Especially when they have been running around playing sweaty scouty games. Ewwww.)

SMELLY Boys

③ The boys leave old bits of gum under the seats.

④ They also leave **Boy** GERMS all over the wooden barre we hold on to when we are doing our *demi-pliés.* (Which is another fancy word for a type of knee-bending exercise.)

Wooden Barre

demi-plié

So anyway, we were all in the middle of our warm-up stretches when Mrs. (I mean *Madame*) Fry announced that she had an important

announcement to make. Of course we all wanted to know IMMEDIATELY what the important announcement was going to be. But Madame Fry said we had to wait until the end of class. And that she would only tell us if we had all worked really hard with NO SLACKING OFF.

So then we had to finish off our warm-up stretching, do all the knee-bendy *plié* things

at the *barre*, and practice
all our leaps and jumps
and twirls across the floor
(my favorite part) before we
could find out. Mrs. Radinsky
(who is about 896 years old)
played tinkly music on the
piano (which is even older)
while Madame Fry walked
around the room putting
our legs and arms in the
right place or checking
to see our backs were straight
and our bottoms tucked in.

Knee-
Bendy
Plié

Leaps

Jumps

twirls

Sticking your bottom out in ballet is the WORST THING YOU CAN POSSIBLY DO.

← Head poked forward

← Round SHOULDERS

→ Bottom stuck out

straight Back AND Head

Bottom tucked in

Then she said we had to wait until we'd
completed our warm-down stretches before
she revealed her important announcement.
By then of course everyone
was getting really twitchy,
busting to know what it was.
There was Madame Fry telling
us to be CALM, CALM,
CALM, when actually we were
all CRAZY, CRAZY, CRAZY,
buzzing like little ballet bees
trapped in a bottle. Especially Zoe and
me. We LOVE important announcements
(especially if they
have anything to do
with chocolate cake).

BUZZ

BUZZszz

("   ")

Ballet
Bees trapped
IN A BOTTLE!

Chocolate
CAKE!

(yum Yum!)

Then, finally, we stretched our last stretch and it was time! Madame Fry turned to us, her eyes shining like twin twinkly stars, and said:

Madame
FRY

"Everyone, I have something VERY, VERY exciting to tell you."

We all turned to each other, our eyes shining like ~~76~~ ~~92~~ a sky full of twinkly stars, wondering what the exciting thing might be.

Possible EXCITING things MADAME was about TO TELL US:

⚙ ① Our *École du Ballet* has been discovered by a famous movie producer, and we are all about to become famous movie stars.

② A pop star wants us all to appear as dancers in his next video clip.

③ Mrs. Radinsky is going to retire.

4 A ballet shoe company has decided to award us all ~~$500~~ $10,000 dance scholarships and give us ballet shoes forever and ever.

5 An advertising company needs two brilliant dancers who look just like Zoe and me to appear in a TV commercial for chocolate cake.

yum

Ella AND ZOE

appear in
CHOCOLATE CAKE
commercial!

And then Madame Fry told us **that** . . .

Read them all!